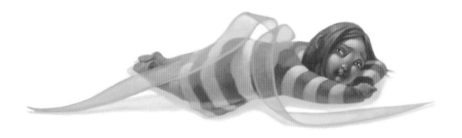

PETER PAN

PETER PAN

From the story by J. M. Barrie

Illustrated by Patricia Castelao Costa

RP | KIDS
PHILADELPHIA • LONDON

For Marcos and our little Claudia,
with all my love.

Many thanks to Justin and Frances for their support.

—P.C.

Cover design by Frances J. Soo Ping Chow
Interior design by Mary Ann Ackerman
Typography: Bembo Titling and ITC Berkeley
Adaptation by Brooke Lindner
Edited by T.L. Bonaddio

Published by Running Press Kids, an imprint of
Running Press Book Publishers
2300 Chestnut Street
Philadelphia, PA 19103-4371

Visit us on the web!
www.runningpress.com

r. and Mrs. Darling were getting ready to go out for the evening. Mrs. Darling was dressed in a beautiful white dress while Mr. Darling was dressed in a dark suit. They came to say good night to their children—Wendy, Michael, and John. Mr. Darling wanted to be exactly like his neighbors. They couldn't afford a "real" nanny for their children so they had a dog for one. Her name was Nana. The children and Mrs. Darling just loved Nana but Mr. Darling felt otherwise—especially on this particular night. Nana was nervous that Mr. and Mrs. Darling were leaving and wouldn't stop barking.

Nana brushed up against Mr. Darling and unintentionally ruined his suit. "I refuse to allow this dog to run my house anymore," Mr. Darling exclaimed. He felt like the proper place for Nana was in the yard. When he tried to put her there, the children cried and hugged Nana but Mr. Darling was determined to prove a point.

"George, remember what I told you about that boy, Peter Pan," Mrs. Darling whispered to her husband.

Mrs. Darling was getting at an incident that happened the week before. Wendy, the oldest child of the three had told Mrs. Darling about a boy that visited them every night named Peter Pan. Peter lived with fairies in a place called Neverland.

"What nonsense you talk, precious. No one can get into this house without knocking," Mrs. Darling said to her daughter.

"I think he can fly, mother," Wendy said. Mrs. Darling didn't want to believe her daughter, but she couldn't help think of her own memory as a young girl. She remembered a boy named Peter Pan in her dreams who said he lived with fairies, but he would have been grown up by now.

That night, something spectacular happened. While the children slept, Nana and Mrs. Darling saw that very young boy appear in the middle of the bedroom. He was dressed in leaves and was the same size and age of Wendy. But before they could catch Peter, he flew out the window. Nana was, however, able to grab his shadow which Mrs. Darling tucked away in a dresser drawer.

While Mr. Darling acknowledged that Nana had done some good the week before by grabbing Peter's shadow, he insisted that she spend the night outside. Nana barked in protest, but Mr. Darling in his fit of fury took her away.

When things calmed down, Mrs. Darling tucked her children back into bed and sang them a lullaby. They could hear Nana barking.

"It is because father has chained her up," John whimpered.

"No, John. That is Nana's bark when she smells *danger*," Wendy demanded.

Mrs. Darling shooshed her children but made sure that the nursery's window was secured tighter than usual.

"Can anything harm us, mother?" the youngest child, Michael, cried.

"Nothing, precious," Mrs. Darling said. "The nightlights are the eyes a mother leaves behind to make sure that her children are safe and sound."

Mrs. Darling really wished she could stay with her children instead of going out with Mr. Darling to another one of his work parties. But, nonetheless, they were going to be a few doors down, so she hugged her children goodbye and wished them sweet dreams. Those were the last words she would say to them for a very long time.

Once Mr. and Mrs. Darling left, the children fell asleep. The window flew open and a light that was a thousand times brighter than a "normal" nightlight appeared. It was a fairy looking for Peter Pan's shadow. Her name was Tinker Bell. Behind Tinker Bell was Peter Pan.

"Tink, where are you?" Peter Pan called softly from the nursery's window. A tinkle of golden bells answered him and said that Peter's shadow was in the top drawer of a chest. Peter jumped to the drawer where he found his shadow. He tried to stick it on him but it wouldn't stay. Peter sobbed and sobbed for he never wanted his shadow as much as he wanted it now.

His sobs woke Wendy. "Why are you crying?" she asked Peter.

"I'm crying because I can't get my shadow to stick."

"That's it?" Wendy asked. "I can fix it for you just by sewing it on." As Wendy went to find a needle and thread, she asked Peter where he was from.

"Second to the right and then straight on until morning," Peter said as he pointed out the window to the stars in the sky.

"What a funny address," Wendy said. "How does your mother get any letters?" Wendy asked.

"I don't have a mother."

And Peter didn't want one. Wendy couldn't believe it and thought he should be crying about not having a mother instead of losing his shadow.

"Wendy, I ran away the day I was born." Peter said. He didn't want to grow up so he lived among fairies.

To prove that he was telling the truth, Peter wanted to show Wendy a real fairy, Tinker Bell, but couldn't find her anywhere.

"Do you hear her?" Peter asked. The only sound Wendy heard was a tinkle of bells. The sound was coming from the top drawer of the chest. Peter had accidentally shut the drawer on Tink when he found his shadow. He let the fairy out and she flew around the nursery screaming with fury.

"Oh, Tink. I am so sorry," Peter said. Wendy just wanted Tink to stop moving for one second so she could see her. Wendy never saw a fairy before.

"This lady wishes you were her fairy," Peter said to Tink. But Tinker Bell was not very fond of Wendy. She was Peter's fairy and didn't like the fact that another girl was talking to him. Tink was very upset and flew away to the bathroom.

Wendy was enthralled by her new friend, Peter, and had so many questions to ask. "Well, where do you and the rest of the fairies live?"

"I live in Neverland with the Lost Boys—children who never want to grow up just like me," Peter said. There were no girls or mothers in Neverland and Peter wished that there were more so they could hear bedtime stories.

Peter then gave Wendy an acorn which was equivalent to a kiss in Neverland.

Wendy put the acorn on a string and tied it around her neck. Tinker Bell saw this and it made her so mad that she pulled Wendy's hair!

"I've never seen you as naughty as you are right now," Peter said to Tinker Bell.

Peter went to fly away but Wendy begged him not to leave. "Then come with me to tell stories to the Lost Boys," Peter said.

"I can't leave my brothers, Peter," Wendy said. "And, besides, I can't fly."

Peter said he would teach Wendy to fly and that her brothers could also come. Wendy ran and woke up Michael and John.

"How do you fly?" John asked Peter in amazement. Then Peter told them the secret to learning how to fly.

"You just think wonderful thoughts," Peter explained. "And then you fly." Peter made flying look so easy! Wendy, John, and Michael all thought of their favorite things. Wendy thought of books. John thought of pirates. Michael thought of his favorite stuffed animal. But as much as the Darling children tried thinking about all of their most favorite and wonderful things, they still couldn't fly.

Peter then told the three Darling children the *real* secret to flying—fairy dust! He blew some fairy dust on each of them and asked them to wiggle their shoulders and let go.

"Look at me!" Michael yelled as he flew across the room. In an instant, the three children were up in the air. They weren't as elegant as Peter, but they were flying!

"Let's fly out of the nursery," Peter said. "Come with me to Neverland where there are mermaids, pirates, and the Lost Boys."

Nana saw the three children in the air and barked as loudly as she could to get Mr. and Mrs. Darling's attention. But it didn't matter—they were gone.

Peter led the way on their journey to Neverland. The Darling children were delighted as they flew above their city over hills and mountains and across two oceans. But after the third day of flying, they were tired and hungry and ready to land.

"There it is," Peter said calmly as he pointed to an island below. Wendy, John, and Michael tiptoed in the air to get their first sight of Neverland. Everything looked

really familiar to them. The island looked like something that was taken right from their dreams. There was a lagoon and a native camp for John. And a cave for Michael. And wolf puppies for Wendy.

There were three groups in Neverland—the Lost Boys, the natives of Neverland, and the pirates. The pirates were enemies against both groups. The natives and the Lost Boys left each other alone but they weren't friends. The only thing they had in common was that they both hated the pirates.

Peter asked the Darling children if they wanted to go on a pirate adventure.

"There's a pirate asleep right down there," Peter said. "Let's go down there and scare him."

"How many pirates are down there?" Michael asked. Peter said there were tons of pirates. They were nothing to be scared of, except for their captain—Hook.

"He has an iron hook on his left hand because of me!" Peter said with pride.

"You must promise me that if we ever meet Hook, you will leave him to me." The children promised.

———■———

Captain Hook and his sidekick Smee were in the forest in Neverland. Smee would do anything that Hook wanted him to do. But without Hook, Smee didn't have much courage. They were looking for the entrance to the underground home in the forest, where Peter and the Lost Boys lived. Of course, Peter made sure that the pirates could never enter his home. All of the trees looked the same to Hook and Smee but seven of them had a special doorway for each of the Lost Boys and Peter to enter.

There were six Lost Boys that lived with Peter. First was gullible Tootles and then there was happy-go-lucky Nibs. And next was Slightly who was the most conceited. Then there was Curly who always got into trouble unintentionally. And last but not least were the twins who acted like one person instead of two.

"I want their captain, Peter Pan," Hook said to Smee. "He cut off my hand and I've waited a long time to get my revenge."

Years before, Peter and Hook had a sword fight and Peter prevailed and won. In the end, he had flung Hook's hand to a crocodile and ever since that day, that crocodile followed Hook from sea to land licking his lips. It swallowed a clock that was found in the sea, instead of all of Hook. And that clock *tick tick ticked,* telling Hook whenever the crocodile was near.

"Did you hear that Peter Pan has been away for three days?" Smee asked Hook.

"Oh, really," Hook said slyly. "Let's leave the forest and go to the shore of the Mermaid's Lagoon. We'll leave a poisonous cake for the Lost Boys to eat. This will show Peter who's the leader of this island."

Hook gloated and laughed at his plan. Then he heard *tick tick tick*—the infamous sound of the crocodile—and shuddered in fright.

"Back to the ship, Smee!" Hook ordered. "Jolly Roger, here we come!"

As soon as things were quiet, the Lost Boys came out from underground. They tricked those pirates yet again—Peter would be so proud. They missed him terribly. Three days was a long time for the Lost Boys to be without a leader. They looked forward to when he would come home. Peter would tell them stories that he heard from the bedroom window of that girl who lived so far away.

"W"e're almost home," Peter said. "Neverland is right down—"

Bang!

Because of Tinker Bell's light, Peter and the Darling children were spotted by the pirates on the Jolly Roger who fired at them. No one was hit, but they were blown away in different directions. Tinker Bell lured Wendy in her direction. Wendy didn't realize, though, that Tink was leading her to her doom.

The Lost Boys saw the spark in the sky and as they looked up, they saw a beautiful white bird.

"What kind of bird do you think it is?" Nibs asked. And at that moment, Tink flew down and whispered to the boys, "It's a Wendy, and Peter wants you to shoot her!"

Tinker Bell really wasn't that bad. She was just very jealous of all of the attention that Peter gave to Wendy.

"Out of the way, Tink," gullible Tootles said. And he fired an arrow straight at Wendy.

Wendy fell to the ground. When she landed, the Lost Boys realized that it was not a bird, but a girl. They realized that Peter must have brought the girl to Neverland to take care of them.

"I killed her," Tootles trembled and tried to run away. He was afraid of what Peter would say.

"Let's hide her," the Lost Boys said, but they didn't have the time.

"Greetings, boys," Peter said as he gracefully landed in front of his clan. The boys saluted him but wouldn't say a word.

"Why are you not cheering?" Peter asked. "Anyway, I have fantastic news— I brought a mother home for you." It was the same girl that told Peter all of the stories and he couldn't wait for the Lost Boys to meet her.

"Peter, something has happened to this mother that you are talking about," Tootles glumly said. "I will show her to you."

The boys all stood back as Tootles explained that he shot her. Peter was so angry, but then Wendy's arm moved. The arrow went into the acorn kiss that Peter gave her. Wendy was in a deep sleep but she was alive!

In the distance, Peter heard a cry of defeat from Tinker Bell. Peter realized what Tink had done.

"I am no longer your friend!" Peter yelled. Tink flew onto Peter's shoulder and pleaded, but he brushed her off. Then Wendy moved her arm again. "Well, not forever. But for a whole week."

To show how sorry they were, the Lost Boys decided to build a house around Wendy while she slept. John and Michael helped the Lost Boys as well. They all waited for Wendy to get up from this deep sleep.

When she finally awoke she asked, "Where am I?" The boys told her that she was in Neverland and that she was now their mother.

"But I am only a little girl," Wendy said. "I can't be your mother."

"That doesn't matter, Wendy," Peter explained. "We just need a nice motherly person."

"I will do my best," Wendy said. "Before I put you to bed, I will tell you all a wonderful story."

The boys perked up and spent the first of many wonderful nights listening to Wendy tell them spectacular stories about princesses and princes and how they lived happily ever after.

The next morning, Peter Pan measured Wendy, John, and Michael for hollow trees so they could come and go as they pleased. The trees were the only way to enter underground.

The Darling children just loved their new home. Wendy fell right into her new role as mother of the Lost Boys. She cooked them grand meals—although she never knew if it was going to be a real meal or just make-believe.

The Lost Boys could eat, really eat, but if there wasn't enough food to eat, the next best thing was to use their imagination and talk about glorious dinners. They would just think of their favorite foods and suddenly they would appear. Anything could happen in Neverland.

Wendy's favorite time was when all of the boys went to bed, since this was the only time that she had to herself. The Lost Boys and her brothers could be quite a handful. Sometimes she sewed patches on the knees of their pants and sometimes she would just think.

One thing that always crossed her mind was her mother and father. Wendy missed her parents but she was absolutely sure that they would keep the window open in the nursery for her and her brothers to fly back home.

Wendy made sure that she reminded her brothers of home as much as she could. But sometimes John and Michael would forget about their mother and father.

Wendy decided to give them tests with such questions as "What was the color of Mother's eyes?" "Write an essay on how you spent Christmas last year," or "Describe Father's laugh." Some of the Lost Boys would participate as well and they would

try to describe their own mothers and fathers—or at least what they could remember of them. There was only one person who would never participate in this activity and that was Peter. He couldn't write, read, or spell and only liked one mother, and that was Wendy.

Neverland was always filled with fun and adventure. One day, Peter, Wendy, John, Michael, and the Lost Boys had finished a long day of swimming and relaxing at the Mermaid's Lagoon. They were all resting on Marooner's Rock when John noticed a small rowboat with three figures approaching them.

In the boat were two pirates—Smee and Starkey—and a prisoner, Tiger Lily, who was the chief natives' daughter! The pirates had caught Tiger Lily trying to board the Jolly Roger and as punishment Captain Hook banished her to Marooner's Rock. Hook ordered Smee and Starkey to take her there and he would stay at the Jolly Roger. Tiger Lily was only trying to get on the boat out of curiosity, but Hook wouldn't hear her pleas. And he warned Smee and Starkey that if they came back with Tiger Lily, he would banish them too.

Hook didn't believe that the pirates would finish the deed. He would check up on them later.

The pirates were coming closer and closer to Marooner's Rock, so Peter ordered the Lost Boys to hide underneath the water. They were all great swimmers. Peter and Wendy were on the other side of Marooner's Rock so they could hear the pirate's conversation but the pirates couldn't see them.

"Okay, Starkey." Smee said. "All we have to do is use this rope to tie the girl on the rock so she'll drown by dusk."

Wendy was softly crying but then Peter had a brilliant idea. He would pretend to be the voice of Captain Hook.

"Set her free," bellowed Peter to the pirates.

"Captain, is all well?" Smee asked timidly. The two pirates were very curious to know what had brought their captain to them.

"I changed my mind about Tiger Lily," Peter said.

"Better to do what the captain orders," said Starkey nervously.

"Ay, ay," Smee said, as he cut the ropes off of Tiger Lily's hands. Tiger Lily jumped into the water and swam away from Marooner's Rock as fast as she could—she was free.

At that exact moment, they all heard the *real* voice of Captain Hook. He went to Marooner's Rock to check up on Smee and Starkey. Peter and Wendy were listening in on their conversation.

"I came to not only check in on you but to let you know of another stupendous idea that I have," Hook said.

"We're all ears," Smee said.

"The Lost Boys have found a mother and her name is Wendy," Hook said. "She also has two brothers who are always protecting her." He told the pirates that he would make the Lost Boys, Michael, and John walk the plank on the Jolly Roger. Hook would let Wendy survive so that she could be the mother of all of the pirates.

Smee and Starkey clapped at their captain's idea. And Wendy, who was hiding right behind Marooner's Rock listening to their scheme, gasped.

"What was that?" Hook asked in response to Wendy's gasp. Peter pulled Wendy beneath the water.

"I heard nothing," said Starkey.

Suddenly, Hook remembered why he went to Marooner's Rock. "Now, where is Tiger Lily?" asked Hook.

"Um, we let her go just like you said," Smee answered. Hook's face went red with rage.

"Lads, I gave no such orders," Hook said.

"But we heard you, sir," Smee begged nervously.

And then Peter who was hiding underneath the water couldn't control himself and said, "I am James Hook, captain of the Jolly Roger." Peter started laughing at his own game.

Hook recognized Peter's laugh instantly. "Peter Pan, you are mine!" Hook screamed as he looked around to see where the voice was coming from. But Peter was not alone in this fight against Hook.

Here and there, the heads of the Lost Boys popped out of the water. John, Michael, and Slightly fought Starkey. And Tootles and the twins dunked Smee in the water.

While the fight between the pirates and the Lost Boys continued in the water, Peter seeked out Hook. Finally, the captain of the pirates and the leader of the Lost Boys met face to face on top of Marooner's Rock. They were both ready for revenge.

Instantly, Hook bit Peter right in his arm! Peter was sure he was doomed but luck was in his favor. Out of nowhere, they both heard, *tick tick tick*. It was the crocodile! And although revenge against Peter was in Hook's reach, the crocodile was his ultimate enemy. So, with a splash, Hook fled away from Marooner's Rock as fast as he could to get back to the Jolly Roger where he would be safe.

And in all of the commotion, the Lost Boys swam back to shore, far away from Marooner's Rock. But once they got there they realized that Peter and Wendy were both missing.

"Wendy! Peter!" John yelled. But all they heard was their echo.

"Help, help!" Wendy screamed as she tried to stay above the water. Peter swam to her and brought her to Marooner's Rock, but the water was rising.

"Wendy, I can't swim or fly anymore," Peter said faintly, as he grabbed his injured arm from when Hook bit him. And then out of nowhere, Michael's kite had flown right toward them and gently hit Peter's face. It was as if the wind blew the kite to Peter and Wendy to save them. "Wendy, you have to go on this kite," Peter said weakly.

"It can carry both of us, right?" Wendy asked.

"Michael and Curly tried before and it will only take one person," Peter said as he tied the kite tail around Wendy and pushed her from the rock. "Goodbye, Wendy."

Peter was the bravest Lost Boy, but he was scared. The sun was beginning to set and soon it would be dark. He felt so alone—but not for long.

A few moments later, a giant Never bird appeared! She held a nest in her beak and wanted Peter to use it as a boat. Peter took the two eggs that were in the Never bird's nest and put them in his hat for safety. The Never bird was so happy that her babies were safe and promised to watch over Peter forever.

When Peter arrived back to Neverland, the Lost Boys and Wendy rejoiced! They celebrated all night until Wendy realized how late it was.

"Off to bed, boys," she said.

They hesitated a bit but since she was such a great mother, they obeyed.

One important result of saving Tiger Lily from Marooner's Rock was that it made the natives friends of Peter and the Lost Boys. There was nothing that they wouldn't do for them. As for the pirates, though, the natives sat in the forest waiting for them to come for revenge yet again. But Peter was sure that Hook would be too scared to show his face again.

———————■———————

he next day, the Lost Boys, Michael, John, Peter, and Wendy were all sitting around a table having make-believe tea. They looked like a family with Peter and Wendy as the parents.

"I was just thinking," said Peter. "It is only make-believe that I am their father, isn't it?"

"But they are ours, Peter—yours and mine," Wendy replied.

"But not really, Wendy?" Peter asked.

"Not if you don't wish it," Wendy said with a bit of sadness. Wendy wished more than anything that she could be the mother of all of these children and that Peter would think of her as a wife.

But instead of telling Peter how she felt, Wendy proceeded to read a wonderful story to all of her children. It was a story about Mr. and Mrs. Darling.

"I knew them," John said to annoy the others.

"I think I knew them," said Michael rather doubtfully.

Wendy continued her story—the story of how she and her brothers came to Neverland. "One night, Mr. Darling was angry with their dog Nana. He chained her up and then all of the children flew away to where all of the Lost Boys were."

"Oh, Wendy!" cried Tootles. "Was one of the Lost Boys called Tootles?"

"Yes, he was," Wendy said. "But hush and let me finish this story so you can see how the parents who lost their children felt."

"If you knew how great a mother's love is, you would know that she was never afraid," Wendy continued.

This is the part that Peter hated.

"You see Mrs. Darling, the mother, would always leave the window open for her children to fly home," Wendy said.

"Did they ever go back?" Nibs asked.

"They did, Nibs, and they did it all for their mother."

Peter couldn't listen anymore and interrupted Wendy. "You are wrong about mothers," Peter said. All of the Lost Boys gathered around Peter in awe.

"Long ago," he said. "I thought that my mother would always keep the window open for me, but when I flew back, the window was closed. My mother had forgotten all about me. And there was another little boy sleeping in my bed."

"We want to go home," John and Michael said to Wendy.

"Not tonight!" the Lost Boys said in unison.

But Wendy was so afraid that maybe Peter's story was correct. "At once we must go!" she said to her brothers. The Lost Boys didn't want to lose Wendy, the only mother they knew. They wanted to keep her prisoner, but Peter wouldn't keep anyone in Neverland against their will.

"Tinker Bell will take you home," Peter said. "Nibs, wake Tink up for me."

Nibs had to knock twice on Tink's door before he got an answer. Tink had really been up in bed listening for some time.

"What do you want?" Tink cried.

"Get up, Tink," Nibs said. "And take Wendy and her brothers back home."

Of course Tink was excited that Wendy was going home, but she didn't want to have to be the one to take her home.

"No way," Tink answered and pretended to go back to sleep.

But Peter was able to convince Tink otherwise. "Please do this for me," Peter said.

Tink couldn't say no to Peter. "Who said I wasn't getting up?" Tink cried.

The Lost Boys were so sad to lose the only mother they knew.

"If you will all come with me, I am sure my mother and father will adopt you," Wendy said.

The boys rushed to get their things and were dancing with joy.

"Get your things, Peter," Wendy said.

"No," Peter said. "I am perfectly happy here." Wendy tried to convince Peter otherwise but Peter wouldn't budge. The others had to be told.

"Peter isn't coming," Wendy said. The Lost Boys gazed blankly at Peter. Their first thought was that if Peter wasn't going with them, then he'd probably change his mind about letting them go as well.

But Peter was far too proud. "If you find your mothers," he said coolly, "I hope you like them."

"Well if you won't go with us Peter, will you at least remember to take your medicine?" Wendy said as she took Peter's hand.

"Yeah, sure," Peter said underneath his breath. "Lead the way, Tinker Bell, and so long, Wendy. It was great knowing you."

Tink darted from underground to fly away with the children but no one followed her. They heard commotion from above ground—the pirates were attacking the natives!

Around the brave Tiger Lily were a dozen warriors meant to protect her. They stood as still as statues. The natives had fought hard and strong to protect the chief's daughter and the Lost Boys, but, because the pirates' raid was such a surprise, they were defeated.

Hook and his gang were excited about their victory but what they really were looking for was Peter, Wendy, John, Michael, and the Lost Boys. Hook would stop at nothing to get what he wanted, but there was one barrier that was still stopping him—which tree would he need to get into to get underground?

There was silence for quite awhile above ground. Peter wasn't sure who had won the fight—the natives or the pirates? "If the natives won," he said, "then they will beat the drum; it is always their sign of victory."

Just then, Smee had found the natives' drum. "You will never hear this victory drum again," he muttered.

And then Hook had a grand idea. He signed to Smee to beat the drum so that Peter and the Lost Boys would be tricked into thinking that the pirates had lost the battle. Smee chuckled at his leader's idea and hit the drum two times. Hook and his pirates stopped to listen.

"The drum!" Peter cried. "A native victory!"

The doomed Lost Boys answered the drum with a cheer. They said goodbye to Peter since they were now safe to fly away.

The pirates smirked at each other and rubbed their hands. Hook whispered orders to his men, "One man to each tree—now!"

As each Lost Boy came up from the tree, they were flung in a ruthless manner from one pirate to the next. Wendy was treated differently by Hook who raised his hat to her and offered her his arm.

"Good evening, my lady," Hook said. Wendy was too shocked to cry out.

The pirates chained the children together and carried them off to the Jolly Roger.

"Now there's no way you will fly away," Starkey said.

There was only one person left to catch and that was Peter Pan. Hook waited for hours in front of the tree—waiting for Peter to come up—but he did not show. So he decided to enter the tree to capture Peter, now that he knew which tree would bring him underground. Hook tiptoed very slowly and at last, his arch nemesis was found on the bed—sound asleep.

Peter was unaware of the tragedy that had happened above ground. He was so upset that all of the Lost Boys had decided to fly home to be with Wendy and her family, instead of staying with him and never growing old, that he cried himself to sleep.

Hook watched Peter sleep and wondered how he should finish off his enemy. He decided to put four drops of poison in Peter's medicine cup.

"How easy this is," Hook whispered and then turned away from his enemy and escaped.

Peter slept for a few more hours and then heard a soft but cautious knock at his door.

"Who is that?" Peter asked.

There was no answer.

"I won't open unless you speak," Peter cried.

Then at last the visitor spoke.

"Let me in, Peter." It was Tink. Peter opened the door and she flew in excitedly. Her face was flushed and her dress was stained with mud.

"What happened to you?" Peter asked.

"Oh, you could never guess!" she cried. "Wendy and the boys were captured by the pirates!"

"I'll rescue her!" Peter exclaimed. "How mean I was to her. Now look what's happened." As he leapt to grab his sword, he realized that he should take his medicine to make Wendy happy.

"No!" Tink screamed. She had heard Hook mutter about his evil deed of putting poison in Peter's cup as he ran through the forest to get back to the Jolly Roger.

"Why not?" Peter asked.

"It is poisoned by Hook!" Tink said.

"Don't be silly," Peter replied back. "How could he have gotten down here?"

Tinker Bell couldn't explain how Hook did that but all she knew was that the cup was poisoned. Peter raised the cup to drink the medicine. But Tink was too fast for Peter. She got to the cup to drink it before he could.

"Tink, what is the matter with you?" Peter asked.

Tinker Bell drank the poison to prove her love to Peter. She would do anything to save Peter—even risk her life. And before Tink could answer, her light faded.

And in a soft whisper Tink said, "Peter, I think I can get well again if children believed in fairies,"

So, even though no children were around, Peter yelled to whoever might be dreaming of fairies.

"Do you believe?" he cried.

Tink sat up in bed and listened.

"Clap your hands if you believe." And enough children clapped to save Tink. First her voice grew stronger, then she popped out of bed, and she flashed her light through the room more and merrier than ever.

"And now since you are saved, Tink—I must rescue Wendy!"

He had taught the Lost Boys and Wendy a great survival lesson—to leave a mark on the trail wherever they were going so they could find their way back. For instance, Slightly would cut a mark in a tree, Curly would drop seeds, John would leave his hat, and Michael would leave his kite on an important landmark. So as Peter walked through the forest he looked for some sign of how the children were taken to the Jolly Roger, since all of their footsteps were covered by snow.

Peter wandered for miles. He was sure someone would have left something for him. And that's when he saw Wendy's handkerchief hanging on a tree. He was going the right way! Peter was on a mission to not only save Wendy and the Lost Boys but to seek his revenge on the captain of the pirates for the very last time. "Hook or me this time," he promised.

Back on the Jolly Roger, Hook was in pure bliss—he had beaten the fight against the natives, kidnapped Wendy to be a mother for the pirates, finally won in the battle against Peter, and now all of the Lost Boys were about to walk the plank.

"Six of you will walk the plank tonight, but I have room on my ship for two cabin boys," Hook said. "Which of you will it be?"

Tootles stepped forward politely. "You see, sir, I don't think my mother would like me to be a pirate."

"I don't think my mother would like that either," Slightly said.

And then the twins said the same thing.

"Oh, quiet," Hook said and then addressed Wendy's brother, John. "You look as if you would want to be a pirate."

"Actually, I once thought of calling myself Red-handed Jack," he said to Hook.

"That's a good name, son," Hook said. "We'll call you that if you join the pirates."

"What do you think, Michael?" John asked. Michael was impressed and would do whatever his older brother told him to do.

"What would you call me if I join?" Michael asked.

"Blackbeard Joe," Hook said. "You both were born to be on my ship."

Wendy was horrified that her brothers would become pirates.

"No way, boys!" she screamed.

"We refuse," John said. He didn't want to disappoint his sister.

"Then get the plank ready!" Hook said.

"Are they to die?" Wendy asked faintly.

"They are," Hook snarled. "But if you will be our mother, you will be saved."

"I would rather have no children at all," Wendy said firmly.

"Then off to the plank you go!" Hook said. And then he heard the terrible *tick tick tick* of the crocodile.

"The crocodile is about to board the ship!" Hook screamed at Smee and Starkey. "Hide me!"

The pirates took Hook away and left the boys standing on the plank. The Lost Boys rushed to the side of the ship to see the crocodile climbing it. But it wasn't a crocodile that was saving them—it was Peter Pan.

Peter signed to the Lost Boys to not say a peep. Then he went into the cabin of the ship to do four things: defeat the pirates, find the key that would unlock the chains on the Lost Boys, John and Michael, save Wendy, and last but not least—destroy Hook once and for all.

Slowly Hook came out of the cabin to see if he could hear the ticking from the crocodile.

"It's gone, captain," Smee said.

"Then let's get these boys to officially walk the plank!" Hook exclaimed. But before this would happen, Hook wanted his black cat from the cabin so each of the Lost Boys could pet it before they sank into their doom. It would be bad luck for the pirates if their prisoners wouldn't pet the cat.

"What in the world is going on?" Hook asked. Each pirate that went into the cabin never came out. Little did he know that Peter was hiding in the cabin waiting

patiently for each pirate to meet their doom. First was Jukes, then Cecco, and next was Starkey—Peter killed each pirate off one by one. The Lost Boys wanted to cheer but they couldn't give away their hero!

"They do say that the surest sign that a ship is cursed is when there's one extra person on board," Cookson replied.

"Oh, quiet yourself," Hook said. "Let us all go in the cabin."

Peter ran out of the cabin before the pirates could see him. He secretly cut Wendy's ropes.

"Hide with the other Lost Boys, Wendy," Peter whispered, as he gave her the key to unlock their chains. He took Wendy's place and disguised himself as her by wearing her coat. Then he took a great big breath and crowed.

Hook came out of the cabin as soon as he heard the crow. He was in shock that three of his men were dead. He looked at Wendy (who was really Peter) with curiosity.

"Quiet, boys," Hook said. "I know what the problem is—we have a woman on board."

The pirates made a rush at the figure in the cloak. "I am going to fling the girl overboard," cried Hook. "There's nothing you can do now to save yourself."

"There's one," replied the figure.

"Who's that?" Hook asked.

"Peter Pan!" said the voice. And in that moment, Peter flung off the cloak to reveal himself. Hook wiped his eyes in disbelief and wondered why the poison didn't do the trick—he was sure that this was an awful dream.

"Get them boys!" Peter screamed. The Lost Boys clashed their swords and went after every remaining pirate until they were all thrown overboard. There was only one pirate left and it was Hook. The Lost Boys all surrounded him with their swords.

"Put down your swords, boys," cried Peter. "Hook is mine." And yet again, the two enemies looked at each other face to face. The other boys drew back and formed a ring around Peter and Hook.

"So, Pan," said Hook. "This is all because of you, I see."

"It is all my doing," Peter said sternly.

"Well, prepare to meet your doom," Hook said.

Hook and Pan lunged at each other—their swords clashing in mid-air. The match was close but Peter fought fiercely. He was a skilled sword fighter and pierced Hook in the ribs. Hook fell down and was at Peter's mercy.

"Now!" cried all the boys, but Peter wouldn't win the match this way. He invited Hook to get up and pick up his sword.

They fought again but Hook weakened. Peter slowly advanced toward Hook and in a last effort knocked him into the sea. The infamous crocodile was waiting for Hook.

The Lost Boys, Wendy, John, and Michael cheered for their hero, Peter. They celebrated all through the night. Even Tinker Bell warmed up to Wendy. They had defeated the pirates once and for all!

When they woke up in the morning, Peter took his place as captain. Nibs and John were first and second mate. The rest were sailors. Although they were all celebrating their victory, it was time for Wendy, John, and Michael to go home. The invitation for the other Lost Boys to go home with them was still open.

"I'll take you all home then," Peter said.

———■———

r. and Mrs. Darling were so heartbroken at the loss of their children. They waited everyday in the nursery for them to come home.

"The window must always be left open for them—always, always," they would say. Mr. Darling blamed himself for that night.

"If I wasn't so mean to Nana that night, this would have never happened," Mr. Darling said. He cried himself to sleep in the nursery every night, begging for his babies to come home.

One night while he slept, Peter and Tink flew into the room. Wendy, John, Michael, and the Lost Boys were just a few minutes behind.

"Quick, Tink," Peter whispered. "Close the window! That way Wendy will think that her mother forgot about them and then she can go back to Neverland with us."

In the other room, Peter saw Wendy's mother crying.

"Well, we can't both have her, lady," Peter said soft enough that she couldn't hear. But Peter did have a heart and he couldn't see Mrs. Darling cry anymore.

"Oh, all right," he said. Peter unlatched the window so it would be wide open for the Darling children to come home. "Come on, Tink," he cried.

And then Wendy, John, and Michael flew into the window.

"I think I have been here before," Michael said.

"Of course, you have, silly," John said. "This is your bed."

They saw Mr. Darling sleeping on the floor but didn't want to wake him.

"Let us all slip into our beds," Wendy said. "That way, when Mother comes in, it will be like we were never away."

Mrs. Darling finally came in to wake up her husband. The children waited for her to cry with joy. But even though she saw them, she didn't believe they were there. She thought she was dreaming.

"Mother!" they all cried at once as they ran to her.

"George!" she cried as she wiped her eyes in disbelief. Nana ran in and they all jumped with joy. It was the happiest sight ever.

The rest of the Lost Boys—all six of them—were waiting downstairs. They stood in a row in front of Mrs. Darling with their hats off. They said nothing, but their eyes asked her to take them in as her children, too. Mrs. Darling agreed to take them in right away. It was a dream that came true.

"I am as glad to have them as you are," Mr. Darling said to his wife. "I just wish you would have asked me, too."

"Oh, George," Mrs. Darling said.

"We'll fit in, sir," they assured him. "We promise to be good children."

"Then follow the leader," Mr. Darling cried. "Let's find you some places to sleep!" As Mr. Darling took the Lost Boys to their beds, Mrs. Darling took Wendy, John, and Michael up to their nursery.

Peter came to the nursery's window and said, "Goodbye, Wendy."

"Oh, Peter," Wendy said. "Please don't go away—you can stay here."

"I am going to live in the house we built for you with Tink," Peter said. "Why don't you come with me?"

Wendy was so tempted to go. "May I, mother?" Wendy asked. "Peter needs a mother."

"Certainly not," Mrs. Darling said. "You need a mother just as much as he does, my love, and I missed you for way too long."

Wendy and Peter begged for some way to see each other, so Mrs. Darling gave them a splendid offer—Wendy would be allowed to go with Peter for one week once a year.

"You won't forget me, Peter, will you?"

"Never ever," Peter said as he flew away. And that was the last time that Wendy ever saw him.

———■———

ll of the Lost Boys grew up and so did Wendy, John, and Michael. Slightly married a lady and became a lord. Tootles became a judge. John became a doctor. Nibs and Curly became bankers. The twins became teachers. Michael became a train engineer.

And sweet Wendy fell in love with a handsome man and got married.

She had a daughter named Jane who loved to hear her mother's wonderful stories about Peter and her adventures in Neverland when she was a little girl. Wendy wasn't sure if there was a Neverland anymore—maybe it was just a dream.

"I sometimes wonder, Jane, whether I ever really did fly," Wendy said to her daughter.

That night, Jane was fast asleep in her bed. As Wendy sat on the floor close to the fire, the window blew open. It was Peter—and he was still a little boy.

"Hello, Wendy," he said, not noticing that Wendy was now a woman.

"Hello, Peter," she said faintly.

"I've come to take you to Neverland again," Peter said.

"Peter, I can't go," Wendy said, as she turned on the lights.

"What happened to you, Wendy?" Peter asked.

"I am old, Peter," Wendy said. "I grew up a long time ago."

"But you promised not to," Peter cried.

"I couldn't help it, Peter," Wendy said. And she showed him her daughter, which made Peter cry.

Jane woke up and saw the infamous Peter that her mother had talked so fondly about. She couldn't believe her eyes.

"Why are you crying?" Jane asked—just like her mother did years and years before.

"I came back for my mother," Peter explained to Jane.

"Well, I can be your mother," Jane said.

"This is true, my love. But no one knows how to be Peter's mother as well as I do," Wendy said to her daughter. But Peter would settle for Jane if he couldn't have Wendy. And in that moment, Peter sprinkled fairy dust over Jane.

"Goodbye," said Peter to Wendy as he rose in the air with Jane.

"Oh, how I wish I could go with you," Wendy said.

"But you can't fly anymore," Jane said. And she was right—only little children could fly.

Wendy wanted her baby to have the amazing adventures that she once did, so she let her daughter fly away with Peter.

He would come to the nursery window once a year, every year, to take Wendy's daughter to Neverland. And as the years went by, Peter would return for her granddaughter and then her great granddaughter and so on. He did this always because even boys like Peter Pan who never want to grow up need a mother every once and awhile.

THE END